I0445800

THE EYES OF THAR

Start Publishing PD LLC
Copyright © 2024 by Start Publishing PD LLC

All rights reserved, including the right to reproduce this book or portions
thereof in any form whatsoever.

Start Publishing PD is a registered trademark of Start Publishing PD LLC
Manufactured in the United States of America

Cover art: Shutterstock/Taisiya Kozorez

Cover design: Jennifer Do

10 9 8 7 6 5 4 3 2 1

ISBN 979-8-8809-1555-2

THE EYES OF THAR

by Henry Kuttner

She spoke in a tongue dead a thousand years, and she had no memory for the man she faced. Yet he had held her tightly but a few short years before, had sworn eternal vengeance—when she died in his arms from an assassin's wounds.

He had come back, though he knew what to expect. He had always come back to Klanvahr, since he had been hunted out of that ancient Martian fortress so many years ago. Not often, and always warily, for there was a price on Dantan's head, and those who governed the Dry Provinces would have been glad to pay it. Now there was an excellent chance that they might pay, and soon, he thought, as he walked doggedly through the baking stillness of the night, his ears attuned to any dangerous sound in the thin, dry air.

Even after dark it was hot here. The dead ground, parched and arid, retained the heat, releasing it slowly as the double moons—the Eyes of Thar, in Klanvahr mythology—swung across the blazing immensity of the sky. Yet Samuel Dantan came back to this desolate land as he had come before, drawn by love and by hatred.

The love was lost forever, but the hate could still be satiated. He had not yet glutted his blood-thirst. When Dantan came back to Klanvahr, men died, though if all the men of the Redhelm Tribe were slain, even that could not satisfy the dull ache in Dantan's heart.

Now they were hunting him.

The girl—he had not thought of her for years; he did not want to remember. He had been young when it happened. Of Earth stock, he had during a great Martian drought become godson to an old shaman of Klanvahr, one of the priests who still hoarded scraps of the forgotten knowledge of the past, glorious days of Martian destiny, when bright towers had fingered up triumphantly toward the Eyes of Thar.

Memories ... the solemn, antique dignity of the Undercities, in ruins now ... the wrinkled shaman, intoning his rituals ... very old books, and older stories ... raids by the Redhelm Tribe ... and a girl Samuel Dantan had known. There was a raid, and the girl had died. Such things had happened many times before; they would happen again. But to Dantan this one death mattered very much.

THE EYES OF THAR

Afterward, Dantan killed, first in red fury, then with a cool, quiet, passionless satisfaction. And, since the Redhelms were well represented in the corrupt Martian government, he had become outlaw.

The girl would not have known him now. He had gone out into the spaceways, and the years had changed him. He was still thin, his eyes still dark and opaque as shadowed tarn-water, but he was dry and sinewy and hard, moving with the trained, dangerous swiftness of the predator he was—and, as to morals, Dantan had none worth mentioning. He had broken more than ten commandments. Between the planets, and in the far-flung worlds bordering the outer dark, there are more than ten. But Dantan had smashed them all.

In the end there was still the dull, sickening hopelessness, part loneliness, part something less definable. Hunted, he came back to Klanvahr, and when he came, men of the Redhelms died. They did not die easily.

But this time it was they who hunted, not he. They had cut him off from the aircar and they followed now like hounds upon his track. He had almost been disarmed in that last battle. And the Redhelms would not lose the trail; they had followed signs for generations across the dying tundras of Mars.

He paused, flattening himself against an outcrop of rock, and looked back. It was dark; the Eyes of Thar had not yet risen, and the blaze of starlight cast a ghastly, leprous shine over the chaotic slope behind him, great riven boulders and jutting monoliths, canyon-like, running jagged toward the horizon, a scene of cosmic ruin that every old and shrinking world must show. He could see nothing of his pursuers, but they were coming. They were still far behind. But that did not matter; he must circle—circle—

And first, he must regain a little strength. There was no water in his canteen. His throat was dust-dry, and his tongue felt swollen and leathery. Moving his shoulders uneasily, his dark face impassive, Dantan found a pebble and put it in his mouth, though he knew that would not help much. He had not tasted water for—how long? Too long, anyhow.

*

6

Staring around, he took stock of resources. He was alone—what was it the old shaman had once told him? "You are never alone in Klanvahr. The living shadows of the past are all around you. They cannot help, but they watch, and their pride must not be humbled. You are never alone in Klanvahr."

But nothing stirred. Only a whisper of the dry, hot wind murmuring up from the distance, sighing and soughing like muted harps. Ghosts of the past riding the night, Dantan thought. How did those ghosts see Klanvahr? Not as this desolate wasteland, perhaps. They saw it with the eyes of memory, as the Mother of Empires which Klanvahr had once been, so long ago that only the tales persisted, garbled and unbelievable.

A sighing whisper ... he stopped living for a second, his breath halted, his eyes turned to emptiness. That meant something. A thermal, a river of wind—a downdraft, perhaps. Sometimes these eon-old canyons held lost rivers, changing and shifting their courses as Mars crumbled, and such watercourses might be traced by sound.

Well—he knew Klanvahr.

A half mile farther he found the arroyo, not too deep—fifty feet or less, with jagged walls easy to descend. He could hear the trickle of water, though he could not see it, and his thirst became overpowering. But caution made him clamber down the precipice warily. He did not drink till he had reconnoitered and made sure that it was safe.

And that made Dantan's thin lips curl. Safety for a man hunted by the Redhelms? The thought was sufficiently absurd. He would die—he must die; but he did not mean to die alone. This time perhaps they had him, but the kill would not be easy nor without cost. If he could find some weapon, some ambush—prepare some trap for the hunters—

There might be possibilities in this canyon. The stream had only lately been diverted into this channel; the signs of that were clear. Thoughtfully Dantan worked his way upstream. He did not try to mask his trail by water-tricks; the Redhelms were too wise for that. No, there must be some other answer.

A mile or so farther along he found the reason for the diverted stream. Landslide. Where water had chuckled and rustled along the left-hand branch

7

before, now it took the other route. Dantan followed the dry canyon, finding the going easier now, since Phobos had risen ... an Eye of Thar. "The Eyes of the god miss nothing. They move across the world, and nothing can hide from Thar, or from his destiny."

Then Dantan saw rounded metal. Washed clean by the water that had run here lately, a corroded, curved surface rose dome-shaped from the stream bed.

The presence of an artifact in this place was curious enough. The people of Klanvahr—the old race—had builded with some substance that had not survived; plastic or something else that was not metal. Yet this dome had the unmistakable dull sheen of steel. It was an alloy, unusually strong or it could never have lasted this long, even though protected by its covering of rocks and earth. A little nerve began jumping in Dantan's cheek. He had paused briefly, but now he came forward and with his booted foot kicked away some of the dirt about the cryptic metal.

A curving line broke it. Scraping vigorously, Dantan discovered that this marked the outline of an oval door, horizontal, and with a handle of some sort, though it was caked and fixed in its socket with dirt. Dantan's lips were very thin now, and his eyes glittering and bright. An ambush—a weapon against the Redhelms—whatever might exist behind this lost door, it was worth investigating, especially for a condemned man.

With water from the brook and a sliver of sharp stone, he pried and chiseled until the handle was fairly free from its heavy crust. It was a hook, like a shepherd's crook, protruding from a small bowl-shaped depression in the door. Dantan tested it. It would not move in any direction. He braced himself, legs straddled, body half doubled, and strained at the hook.

Blood beat against the back of his eyes. He heard drumming in his temples and straightened suddenly, thinking it the footsteps of Redhelms. Then, grinning sardonically, he bent to his work again, and this time the handle moved.

Beneath him the door slid down and swung aside, and the darkness below gave place to soft light. He saw a long tube stretching down vertically, with pegs protruding from the metal walls at regular intervals. It made a ladder. The bottom of the shaft was thirty feet below; its diameter was little more than the breadth of a big man's shoulders.

*

He stood still for a moment, looking down, his mind almost swimming with wonder and surmise. Old, very old it must be, for the stream had cut its own bed out of the rock whose walls rose above him now. Old—and yet these metal surfaces gleamed as brightly as they must have gleamed on the day they were put together—for what purpose?

The wind sighed again down the canyon, and Dantan remembered the Redhelms on his track. He looked around once more and then lowered himself onto the ladder of metal pegs, testing them doubtfully before he let his full weight come down. They held.

There might be danger down below; there might not. There was certain danger coming after him among the twisting canyons. He reached up, investigated briefly, and swung the door back into place. There was a lock, he saw, and after a moment discovered how to manipulate it. So far, the results were satisfactory. He was temporarily safe from the Redhelms, provided he did not suffocate. There was no air intake here that he could see, but he breathed easily enough so far. He would worry about that when the need arose. There might be other things to worry about before lack of air began to distress him.

He descended.

At the bottom of the shaft was another door. Its handle yielded with no resistance this time, and Dantan stepped across the threshold into a large, square underground chamber, lit with pale radiance that came from the floor itself, as though light had been poured into the molten metal when it had first been made.

The room—

Faintly he heard a distant humming, like the after-resonance of a bell, but it died away almost instantly. The room was large, and empty except for some sort of machine standing against the farther wall. Dantan was not a technician. He knew guns and ships; that was enough. But the smooth, sleek functionalism of this machine gave him an almost sensuous feeling of pleasure.

How long had it been here? Who had built it? And for what purpose? He could not even guess. There was a great oval screen on the wall above what seemed to be a control board, and there were other, more enigmatic devices.

And the screen was black—dead black, with a darkness that ate up the light in the room and gave back nothing.

Yet there was something—

"Sanfel," a voice said. "Sanfel. Coth dr'gchang. Sanfel—sthan!

"Sanfel ... Sanfel ... have you returned, Sanfel? Answer!"

It was a woman's voice ... the voice of a woman used to wielding power, quiet, somehow proud as the voice of Lucifer or Lilith might have been, and it spoke in a tongue that scarcely half a dozen living men could understand.... A whole great race had spoken it once; only the shamans remembered now, and the shamans who knew it were few. Dantan's godfather had been one. And Dantan remembered the slurring syllables of the rituals he had learned, well enough to know what the proud, bodiless voice was saying.

The nape of his neck prickled. Here was something he could not understand, and he did not like it. Like an animal scenting danger he shrank into himself, not crouching, but withdrawing, so that a smaller man seemed to stand there, ready and waiting for the next move. Only his eyes were not motionless. They raked the room for the unseen speaker—for some weapon to use when the time came for weapons.

His glance came back to the dark screen above the machine. And the voice said again, in the tongue of ancient Klanvahr:

"I am not used to waiting, Sanfel! If you hear me, speak. And speak quickly, for the time of peril comes close now. My Enemy is strong—"

Dantan said, "Can you hear me?" His eyes did not move from the screen.

Out of that blackness the girl's voice came, after a pause. It was imperious, and a little wary.

"You are not Sanfel. Where is he? Who are you, Martian?"

*

Dantan let himself relax a little. There would be a parley, at any rate. But after that—

Words in the familiar, remembered old language came hesitantly to his lips.

"I am no Martian. I am of Earth blood, and I do not know this Sanfel."

"Then how did you get into Sanfel's place?" The voice was haughty now. "What are you doing there? Sanfel built his laboratory in a secret place."

"It was hidden well enough," Dantan told her grimly. "Maybe for a thousand years, or even ten thousand, for all I know. The door has been buried under a stream—"

"There is no water there. Sanfel's home is on a mountain, and his laboratory is built underground." The voice rang like a bell. "I think you lie. I think you are an enemy—When I heard the signal summoning me, I came swiftly, wondering why Sanfel had delayed so long. I must find him, stranger. I must! If you are no enemy, bring me Sanfel!" This time there was something almost like panic in the voice.

"If I could, I would," Dantan said. "But there's no one here except me." He hesitated, wondering if the woman behind the voice could be—mad? Speaking from some mysterious place beyond the screen, in a language dead a thousand years, calling upon a man who must be long-dead too, if one could judge by the length of time this hidden room had lain buried.

He said after a moment, "This place has been buried for a long time. And—no one has spoken the tongue of Klanvahr for many centuries. If that was your Sanfel's language—" But he could not go on with that thought. If Sanfel had spoken Klanvahr then he must have died long ago. And the speaker beyond the screen—she who had known Sanfel, yet spoke in a young, sweet, light voice that Dantan was beginning to think sounded familiar.... He wondered if he could be mad too.

There was silence from the screen. After many seconds the voice spoke again, sadly and with an undernote of terror.

"I had not realized," it said, "that even time might be so different between Sanfel's world and mine. The space-time continua—yes, a day in my world might well be an age in yours. Time is elastic. In Zha I had thought a few dozen—" she used a term Dantan did not understand, "—had passed. But on Mars—centuries?"

"Tens of centuries," agreed Dantan, staring hard at the screen. "If Sanfel lived in old Klanvahr his people are scarcely a memory now. And Mars is dying. You—you're speaking from another world?"

"From another universe, yes. A very different universe from yours. It was only through Sanfel that I had made contact, until now—What is your name?"

"Dantan. Samuel Dantan."

"Not a Martian name. You are from—Earth, you say? What is that?"

"Another planet. Nearer the sun than Mars."

"We have no planets and no suns in Zha. This is a different universe indeed. So different I find it hard to imagine what your world must be like." The voice died.

*

And it was a voice he knew. Dantan was nearly sure of that now, and the certainty frightened him. When a man in the Martian desert begins to see or hear impossibilities, he has reason to be frightened. As the silence prolonged itself he began almost to hope that the voice—the implausibly familiar voice—had been only imagination. Hesitantly he said, "Are you still there?" and was a little relieved, after all, to hear her say,

"Yes, I am here. I was thinking.... I need help. I need it desperately. I wonder—has Sanfel's laboratory changed? Does the machine still stand? But it must, or I could not speak to you now. If the other things work, there may be chance.... Listen." Her voice grew urgent. "I may have a use for you. Do you see a lever, scarlet, marked with the Klanvahr symbol for 'sight'?"

"I see it," Dantan said.

"Push it forward. There is no harm in that, if you are careful. We can see each other—that is all. But do not touch the lever with the 'door' symbol on it. Be certain of that.... Wait!" Sudden urgency was in the voice.

"Yes?" Dantan had not moved.

"I am forgetting. There *is* danger if you are not protected from—from certain vibration that you might see here. This is a different universe, and your Martian physical laws do not hold good between our worlds. Vibration ... light ... other things might harm you. There should be armor in Sanfel's laboratory. Find it."

Dantan glanced around. There was a cabinet in one corner. He went over to it slowly, his eyes wary. He had no intention of relaxing vigilance here simply because that voice sounded familiar....

Inside the cabinet hung a suit of something like space armor, more flexible and skin tight than any he had ever seen, and with a transparent helmet through which vision seemed oddly distorted. He got into the suit carefully, pulling up the rich shining folds over his body, thinking strangely how long time had stood still in this small room since the last time a man had worn it. The whole room looked slightly different when he set the helmet into place. It must be polarized, he decided, though that alone could not account for the strange dimming and warping of vision that was evident.

"All ready," he said after a moment.

"Then throw the switch."

With his hand upon it Dantan hesitated for one last instant of wariness. He was stepping into unknown territory now, and to him the unknown meant the perilous. His mind went back briefly to the Redhelms scouring the canyons above for him. He quieted his uneasy mind with the thought that there might be some weapon in the world of the voice which he could turn against them later. Certainly, without a weapon, he had little to lose. But he knew that weapon or no weapon, danger or not, he must see the face behind that sweet, familiar, imperious voice.

He pressed the lever forward. It hesitated, the weight of milleniums behind its inertia. Then, groaning a little in its socket, it moved.

Across the screen above it a blaze of color raged like a sudden shining deluge. Blinded by the glare, Dantan leaped back and swung an arm across his eyes.

When he looked again the colors had cleared. Blinking, he stared—and forgot to look away. For the screen was a window now, with the world of Zha behind it.... And in the center of that window—a girl. He looked once at her, and then closed his eyes. He had felt his heart move, and a nerve jumped in his lean cheek.

He whispered a name.

Impassively the girl looked down at him from the screen. There was no change, no light of recognition upon that familiar, beloved face. The face of the girl who had died at the Redhelm hands, long ago, in the fortress of Klanvahr.... For her sake he had hunted the Redhelms all these dangerous years. For her sake he had taken to the spaceways and the outlaw life. In a way, for her sake the Redhelms hunted him now through the canyons overhead. But here in the screen, she did not know him.

He knew that this was not possible. Some outrageous trick of vision made the face and the slender body of a woman from another universe seem the counterpart of that remembered woman. But he knew it must be an illusion, for in a world as different as Zha surely there could be no human creatures at all, certainly no human who wore the same face as the girl he remembered.

*

Aside from the girl herself, there was nothing to see. The screen was blank, except for vague shapes—outlines—The helmet, he thought, filtered out more than light. He sensed, somehow, that beyond her stretched the world of Zha, but he could see nothing except the shifting, ever-changing colors of the background.

She looked down at him without expression. Obviously the sight of him had wakened in her no such deep-reaching echoes of emotion as her face woke in him. She said, her voice almost unbearably familiar; a voice sounding from the silence of death over many chilly years,

"Dantan. Samuel Dantan. Earthly language is as harsh as the Klanvahr I learned from Sanfel. Yet my name may seem strange to you. I am Quiana."

He said hoarsely, "What do you want? What did you want with Sanfel?"

"Help," Quiana said. "A weapon. Sanfel had promised me a weapon. He was working very hard to make one, risking much ... and now time has eaten him up—that strange, capricious time that varies so much between your world and mine. To me it was only yesterday—and I still need the weapon."

Dantan's laugh was harsh with jealousy of that unknown and long-dead Martian.

"Then I'm the wrong man," he said roughly. "I've no weapon. I've men tracking me down to kill me, now."

She leaned forward a little, gesturing.

"Can you escape? You are hidden here, you know."

"They'll find the same way I found, up above."

"The laboratory door can be locked, at the top of the shaft."

"I know. I locked it. But there's no food or water here.... No, if I had any weapons I wouldn't be here now."

"Would you not?" she asked in a curious voice. "In old Klanvahr, Sanfel once told me, they had a saying that none could hide from his destiny."

Dantan gave her a keen, inquiring look. Did she mean—herself? That same face and voice and body, so cruelly come back from death to waken the old grief anew? Or did she know whose likeness she wore—or could it be only his imagination, after all? For if Sanfel had known her too, and if Sanfel had died as long ago as he must have died, then this same lovely image had lived centuries and milleniums before the girl at Klanvahr Fortress....

"I remember," said Dantan briefly.

"My world," she went on, oblivious to the turmoil in his mind, "my world is too different to offer you any shelter, though I suppose you could enter it for a little while, in that protective armor that Sanfel made. But not to stay. We spring from soil too alien to one another's worlds.... Even this communication is not easy. And there is no safety here in Zha either, now. Now that Sanfel has failed me."

"I—I'd help you if I could." He said it with difficulty, trying to force the remembrance upon himself that this was a stranger.... "Tell me what's wrong."

She shrugged with a poignantly familiar motion.

"I have an Enemy. One of a lower race. And he—it—there is no word!—has cut me off from my people here in a part of Zha that is—well, dangerous—I can't describe to you the conditions here. We have no common terms to use in speaking of them. But there is great danger, and the Enemy is coming closer—and I am alone. If there were another of my people here to divide the peril I think I could destroy him. He has a weapon of his own, and it is stronger than my power, though not stronger than the power two of my race together can wield. It—it *pulls*. It destroys, in a way I can find no word to say. I had hoped from Sanfel something to divert him until he could be killed. I told him how to forge such a weapon, but—time would not let him do it. The teeth of time ground him into dust, as my Enemy's weapon will grind me soon."

She shrugged again.

"If I could get you a gun," Dantan said. "A force-ray—"

"What are they?"

He described the weapons of his day. But Quiana's smile was a little scornful when he finished.

"We of Zha have passed beyond the use of missile weapons—even such missiles as bullets or rays. Nor could they touch my Enemy. No, we can destroy in ways that require no—no beams or explosives. No, Dantan, you speak in terms of your own universe. We have no common ground. It is a pity that time eddied between Sanfel and me, but eddy it did, and I am helpless now. And the Enemy will be upon me soon. Very soon."

*

She let her shoulders sag and resignation dimmed the remembered vividness of her face. Dantan looked up at her grimly, muscles riding his set jaw. It was almost intolerable, this facing her again in need, and again helpless, and himself without power to aid. It had been bad enough that first time, to learn long afterward that she had died at enemy hands while he was too far away to protect her. But to see it all take place again before his very eyes!

"There must be a way," he said, and his hand gripped the lever marked "door" in the ancient tongue.

"Wait!" Quiana's voice was urgent.

"What would happen?"

"The door would open. I could enter your world, and you mine."

"Why can't you leave, then, and wait until it's safe to go back?"

"I have tried that," Quiana said. "It will never be safe. The Enemy waited too. No, it must come, in the end, to a battle—and I shall not win that fight. I shall not see my own people or my own land again, and I suppose I must face that knowledge. But I did hope, when I heard Sanfel's signal sound again...." She smiled a little. "I know you would help me if you could, Dantan. But there is nothing to be done now."

"I'll come in," he said doggedly. "Maybe there's something I could do."

"You could not touch him. Even now there's danger. He was very close when I heard that signal. This is his territory. When I heard the bell and thought Sanfel had returned with a weapon for me, I dared greatly in coming here." Her voice died away; a withdrawn look veiled her eyes from him.

After a long silence she said, "The Enemy is coming. Turn off the screen, Dantan. And goodbye."

"No," he said. "Wait!" But she shook her head and turned away from him, her thin robe swirling, and moved off like a pale shadow into the dim, shadowless emptiness of the background. He stood watching helplessly, feeling all the old despair wash over him a second time as the girl he loved went alone into danger he could not share. Sometimes as she moved away she was eclipsed by objects he could not see—trees, he thought, or rocks, that did not impinge upon his eyes through the protective helmet. A strange world indeed Zha must be, whose very rocks and trees were too alien for human eyes to look upon in safety.... Only Quiana grew smaller and smaller upon the screen, and it seemed to Dantan as though a cord stretched between them, pulling thinner and thinner as she receded into danger and distance.

It was unbearable to think that the cord might break—break a second time....

Far away something moved in the cloudy world of Zha. Tiny in the distance though it was, it was unmistakably not human. Dantan lost sight of Quiana. Had she found some hiding place behind some unimaginable outcropping of Zha's terrain?

The Enemy came forward.

It was huge and scaled and terrible, human, but not a human; tailed, but no beast; intelligent, but diabolic. He never saw it too clearly, and he was grateful to his helmet for that. The polarized glass seemed to translate a little, as well as to blot out. He felt sure that this creature which he saw—or almost saw—did not look precisely as it seemed to him upon the screen. Yet it was easy to believe that such a being had sprung from the alien soil of Zha. There was nothing remotely like it on any of the worlds he knew. And it was hateful. Every line of it made his hackles bristle.

It carried a coil of brightly colored tubing slung over one grotesque shoulder, and its monstrous head swung from side to side as it paced forward into the screen like some strange and terrible mechanical toy. It made no sound, and its progress was horrible in its sheer relentless monotony.

*

Abruptly it paused. He thought it had sensed the girl's presence, somewhere in hiding. It reached for the coil of tubing with one malformed—hand?

"Quiana," it said—its voice as gentle as a child's.

Silence. Dantan's breathing was loud in the emptiness.

"Quiana?" The tone was querulous now.

"Quiana," the monster crooned, and swung about with sudden, unexpected agility. Moving with smooth speed, it vanished into the clouds of the background, as the girl had vanished. For an eternity Dantan watched colored emptiness, trying to keep himself from trembling.

Then he heard the voice again, gentle no longer, but ringing like a bell with terrible triumph, "*Quiana!*"

And out of the swirling clouds he saw Quiana break, despair upon her face, her sheer garments streaming behind her. After her came the Enemy. It had unslung the tube it wore over its shoulder, and as it lifted the weapon Quiana swerved desperately aside. Then from the coil of tubing blind lightning ravened.

Shattering the patternless obscurity, the blaze of its color burst out, catching Quiana in a cone of expanding, shifting brilliance. And the despair in her eyes was suddenly more than Dantan could endure.

His hand struck out at the lever marked "door"; he swung it far over and the veil that had masked the screen was gone. He vaulted up over its low threshold, not seeing anything but the face and the terror of Quiana. But it was not Quiana's name he called as he leaped.

He lunged through the Door onto soft, yielding substance that was unlike anything he had ever felt underfoot before. He scarcely knew it. He flung himself forward, fists clenched, ready to drive futile blows into the monstrous mask of the Enemy. It loomed over him like a tower, tremendous, scarcely seen through the shelter of his helmet—and then the glare of the light-cone caught him.

It was tangible light. It flung him back with a piledriver punch that knocked the breath from his body. And the blow was psychic as well as physical. Shaking and reeling from the shock, Dantan shut his eyes and fought forward, as though against a steady current too strong to breast very long. He felt Quiana beside him, caught in the same dreadful stream. And beyond the source of the light the Enemy stood up in stark, inhuman silhouette.

He never saw Quiana's world. The light was too blinding. And yet, in a subtle sense, it was not blinding to the eyes, but to the mind. Nor was it light, Dantan thought, with some sane part of his mind. Too late he remembered Quiana's warning that the world of Zha was not Mars or Earth, that in Zha even light was different.

THE EYES OF THAR

Cold and heat mingled, indescribably bewildering, shook him hard. And beyond these were—other things. The light from the Enemy's weapon was not born in Dantan's universe, and it had properties that light should not have. He felt bare, emptied, a hollow shell through which radiance streamed.

For suddenly, every cell of his body was an eye. The glaring brilliance, the intolerable vision beat at the foundations of his sanity. Through him the glow went pouring, washing him, nerves, bone, flesh, brain, in floods of color that were not color, sound that was not sound, vibration that was spawned in the shaking hells of worlds beyond imagination.

It inundated him like a tide, and for a long, long, timeless while he stood helpless in its surge, moving within his body and without it, and within his mind and soul as well. The color of stars thundered in his brain. The crawling foulness of unspeakable hues writhed along his nerves so monstrously that he felt he could never cleanse himself of that obscenity.

And nothing else existed—only the light that was not light, but blasphemy.

Then it began to ebb ... faded ... grew lesser and lesser, until—Beside him he could see Quiana now. She was no longer stumbling in the cone of light, no longer shuddering and wavering in its violence, but standing erect and facing the Enemy, and from her eyes—something—poured.

Steadily the cone of brilliance waned. But still its glittering, shining foulness poured through Dantan. He felt himself weakening, his senses fading, as the tide of dark horror mounted through his brain.

And covered him up with its blanketing immensity.

*

He was back in the laboratory, leaning against the wall and breathing in deep, shuddering draughts. He did not remember stumbling through the Door again, but he was no longer in Zha. Quiana stood beside him, here upon the Martian soil of the laboratory. She was watching him with a strange, quizzical look in her eyes as he slowly fought back to normal, his heart quieting by degrees, his breath becoming evener. He felt drained, exhausted, his emotions cleansed and purified as though by baths of flame.

Presently he reached for the clasp that fastened his clumsy armor. Quiana put out a quick hand, shaking her head.

"No," she said, and then stared at him again for a long moment without speaking. Finally, "I had not known—I did not think this could be done. Another of my own race—yes. But you, from Mars—I would not have believed that you could stand against the Enemy for a moment, even with your armor."

"I'm from Earth, not Mars. And I didn't stand long."

"Long enough." She smiled faintly. "You see now what happened? We of Zha can destroy without weapons, using only the power inherent in our bodies. Those like the Enemy have a little of that power too, but they need mechanical devices to amplify it. And so when you diverted the Enemy's attention and forced him to divide his attack between us—the pressure upon me was relieved, and I could destroy him. But I would not have believed it possible."

"You're safe now," Dantan said, with no expression in voice or face.

"Yes. I can return."

"And you will?"

"Of course I shall."

"We are more alike than you had realized."

She looked up toward the colored curtain of the screen. "That is true. It is not the complete truth, Dantan."

He said, "I love you—Quiana." This time he called her by name.

Neither of them moved. Minutes went by silently.

Quiana said, as if she had not heard him, "Those who followed you are here. I have been listening to them for some time now. They are trying to break through the door at the top of the shaft."

He took her hand in his gloved grasp. "Stay here. Or let me go back to Zha with you. Why not?"

"You could not live there without your armor."

"Then stay."

Quiana looked away, her eyes troubled. As Dantan moved to slip off his helmet her hand came up again to stop him.

"Don't."

"Why not?"

For answer she rose, beckoning for him to follow. She stepped across the threshold into the shaft and swiftly began to climb the pegs toward the surface and the hammering of the Redhelms up above. Dantan, at her gesture, followed.

Over her shoulder she said briefly,

"We are of two very different worlds. Watch—but be careful." And she touched the device that locked the oval door.

It slipped down and swung aside.

*

Dantan caught one swift glimpse of Redhelm heads dodging back to safety. They did not know, of course, that he was unarmed. He reached up desperately, trying to pull Quiana back but she slipped aside and sprang lightly out of the shaft into the cool gray light of the Martian morning.

Forgetting her warning, Dantan pulled himself up behind her. But as his head and shoulders emerged from the shaft he stopped, frozen. For the Redhelms were falling. There was no mark upon them, yet they fell....

She did not stir, even when the last man had stiffened into rigid immobility. Then Dantan clambered up and without looking at Quiana went to the nearest body and turned it over. He could find no mark. Yet the Redhelm was dead.

"That is why you had to wear the armor," she told him gently. "We are of different worlds, you and I."

He took her in his arms—and the soft resilience of her was lost against the stiffness of the protective suit. He would never even know how her body felt, because of the armor between them.... He could not even kiss her—again. He had taken his last kiss of the mouth so like Quiana's mouth, long years ago, and he would never kiss it again. The barrier was too high between them.

"You can't go back," he told her in a rough, uneven voice. "We *are* of the same world, no matter what—no matter how—You're no stranger to me, Quiana!"

She looked up at him with troubled eyes, shaking her head, regret in her voice.

"Do you think I don't know why you fought for me, Dantan?" she asked in a clear voice. "Did you ever stop to wonder why Sanfel risked so much for me, too?"

He stared down at her, his brain spinning, almost afraid to hear what she would say next. He did not want to hear. But her voice went on inexorably.

"I cheated you, Dantan. I cheated Sanfel yesterday—a thousand years ago. My need was very great, you see—and our ways are not yours. I knew that no man would fight for a stranger as I needed a man to fight for me."

He held her tightly in gloved hands that could feel only a firm body in their grasp, not what that body was really like, nothing about it except its firmness. He caught his breath to interrupt, but she went on with a rush.

"I have no way of knowing how you see me, Dantan," she said relentlessly. "I don't know how Sanfel saw me. To each of you—because I needed your help—I wore the shape to which you owed help most. I could reach into your minds deeply enough for that—to mould a remembered body for your eyes. My own shape is—different. You will never know it." She sighed. "You were a brave man, Dantan. Braver and stronger than I ever dreamed an alien could be. I wish—I wonder—Oh, let me go! Let me go!"

She whirled out of his grasp with sudden vehemence, turning her face away so that he could not see her eyes. Without glancing at him again she bent over the shaft and found the topmost pegs, and in a moment was gone.

Dantan stood there, waiting. Presently he heard the muffled humming of a muted bell, as though sounding from another world. Then he knew that there was no one in the ancient laboratory beneath his feet.

He shut the door carefully and scraped soil over it. He did not mark the place. The dim red spot of the sun was rising above the canyon wall. His face set, Dantan began walking toward the distant cavern where his aircar was hidden. It was many miles away, but there was no one to stop him, now.

He did not look back.

www.ingramcontent.com/pod-product-compliance
Lightning Source LLC
Chambersburg PA
CBHW050910120626
46554CB00003B/1117